W9-CCL-432

A Paula Wiseman Book
Simon & Schuster Books for Young Readers
New York   London   Toronto   Sydney   New Delhi

THE WELCOME CHAIR

Written by
Rosemary Wells

Illustrated by
Jerry Pinkney

PREFACE

My father received his American citizenship in 1935. He told me that during his naturalization ceremony, he learned the three great documents of American history: the Bill of Rights, the Declaration of Independence, and the inscription on the Statue of Liberty. He made me memorize these words: Give me your tired, your poor, your huddled masses yearning to breathe free.

"America's door is open to suffering people from foreign lands," my dad told me. "It's America's fundamental generosity of spirit that makes her hold her head high in a world of trouble. And it always will be so."

My father's words were true until recently. Lady Liberty's message is today challenged by those who want to shut that door.

This book is based in part on my own family's legends, as told to me by my grandmother Marguerite Leopold Bamberger and as passed down to her from her grandmother Ruth Seigbert's diary.

R0461000415

In the year 1807, Sam Seigbert is born in the kingdom of Bavaria. He is my great-great-grandfather but will never know it.

Sam's favorite thing to do is carving wooden toys for his little sister, Sara.

His mother says Sam has a gift from God in his hands.

But Sam's father says Sam must study to be a rabbi.

Sam hates studying the Torah in stuffy rooms by the light of a winking candle.

Sam wants the wind in his hair and the smell of horses in the meadow.

He aches to feel a piece of wood and a knife in his hands.

"You will be a rabbi like me, and your grandfather," says Sam's father. "It's settled. You will not work with your hands like a country bumpkin."

Sam doesn't like to argue.

Early one morning, when Sam is sixteen, he cuts off his sidelocks so that no one will yank them and bully him for being a Jewish boy.

Sam kisses his sleeping mother. She wakes for a moment and sweeps his cheek with her hand. She knows he is leaving without him saying a word. *Please, God, may I see my beautiful boy again,* whisper the fingertips that touch his face.

Sam hikes north through the ancient kingdoms of Mecklenburg and Kassel. His compass is the sun. He keeps it to the right in the mornings and to the left in the afternoons. He walks for three months until he reaches the port of Hamburg.

There, he finds work as a deckhand on a freighter for three pfennigs a day.

Before he sets sail Sam sits on a bollard and writes to his family, telling them the name of his ship and where he is going. The captain of the ship peers over Sam's shoulder.

"You can read and write, boy?" he asks.

Sam is suddenly made keeper of the ship's log and inventory for five pfennigs a day.

Sam's writing finger turns blue with ink, but it means Sam doesn't have to scale the rigging and reef the sails in stormy weather. He won't be tossed like a rag doll into the sea. Sam learns that reading and writing have value in the world. Six weeks later they sail into New York Harbor.

There is a lighthouse at Sandy Hook, but Lady Liberty is not going to appear for another sixty-two years. Sam shakes hands with the captain and then darts away across the Brooklyn docks into the screeching, shrieking, filthy, clanging, terrifying, ugly, and beautiful young city of New York.

Sam walks until he finds Hinzler's Housewright shop on Charlton Street.
"Guten Tag!" says Sam to Able Hinzler. *"Haben Sie arbeit für mich?"*
Klara, Able's wife, notices the blue ink stain on Sam's writing finger.
"Be our bookkeeper?" she blurts out. "Able is a *Hanswurst* with numbers!"

Sam becomes both bookkeeper and apprentice carpenter. When tiny
Magnus Hinzler is born, Sam makes a cherrywood rocking chair for Klara to
sit in comfortably with Magnus. He carves the German word for "Welcome,"
"Willkommen," across a panel, welcoming Magnus into the world.

One year later Able slips and spins off an icy roof. He is unable to work.

Klara's brother writes from Wisconsin. *Come west!* the letter says.

Klara, Able, Magnus, Sam, and pussycat Magda board a brand-new Erie Canal boat that travels through the canal to Buffalo on Lake Erie.

They travel by wagon train the rest of the way to Prairie du Chien on the Mississippi River. The rocking chair goes with them.

Sam, strong and able, goes to work as a carpenter in a joinery.

One evening he finds a young woman singing and peeling the supper potatoes with Klara. Her name is Ruth. She sings like an angel. She also limps.

"I have a clubfoot," says Ruth, "so I came to America. In the old country, no man will marry a woman like me because they think she will have sons who won't walk or work."

Sam falls in love with Ruth's gentle laugh and green-gray eyes.

He makes Ruth a lamb's-wool-lined boot, with wheels, so that Ruth will glide.

They marry. Their first born is Henry. Sam carves "Baruch Haba"—Hebrew for "Welcome"—right under "Willkommen," into the chair's panel so that Henry will know his heritage.

In 1861, the Civil War comes to America. Henry joins the Union Army because he hates slavery and because all the other boys are joining up too.

Sam, Ruth, and their family wave goodbye from their front porch.

The Welcome Chair is brought out to wait for Henry's return.

Helen, Henry's little sister, says, "We are in America now, not Germany!"

She makes her father carve "Welcome" in English into the chair.

Sam sleeps with the wooden toys he carved long ago for Henry under his pillow.

But Henry does not come home. He is killed at Gettysburg in 1863.
The Welcome Chair comes inside at last. It stays in Sam and Ruth's parlor.
Spring breezes tip it gently, as do winter drafts.
No one is allowed to sit in it, in case Henry miraculously comes home.

In 1880, Helen Seigbert elopes with Harry Leopold. They move to New York City to a big fancy house. The chair is sent east by railway. Harry says the Welcome Chair looks like a slice of the prairie. The chair goes up to the sewing room and is draped with chintz and bombazine.

Lucy Kennedy is Irish. She comes to the United States with her mam and da when she is two because people in Ireland are starving. As a child Lucy has to work twelve hours a day spooling thread in a thread factory. All the same, Lucy learns fine sewing by gaslight.

Helen Leopold hires Lucy as the family seamstress. Lucy mends clothing and sews beautiful dresses while rocking in the Welcome Chair. When Lucy marries the doorman at The Plaza Hotel, Helen Leopold gives them the chair as a wedding present. First she orders brass letters for it, spelling "*Fáilte*"—Irish for "Welcome."

In the years to come, Lucy treasures the chair as do all her children.

The chair is their locomotive, their stagecoach, their battleship.

They wreck it.

Broken and splintered, the chair winds up on the sidewalk for the junk man.

Luckily, a Salvation Army antique cart stops first.

In 1939, Sister Carlotta and Sister Emmanuel are best friends in the Dominican city of Santo Domingo. They join a nursing convent together. They heal the wounds and sickness of the poor.

The Dominican Republic is ruled by a dictator, Rafael Trujillo.

He murders anyone who disagrees with him, and terrifies his citizens.

He places his name above God's name on the churches.

The sisters object. They write letters.

They go up on a ladder to change the words in front of the church.

Trujillo's secret police catch them taking down the dictator's name. They tell them they will be severely punished unless they stop making trouble. They are thrown in jail.

But a prison guard's little daughter has an infected boil. She is close to dying of blood poisoning. Sister Emmanuel treats the boil with sulfa powder, and it heals. The guard unlocks their cell. The sisters dress quickly in their black habits and race away, unseen in the moonlight.

Hidden in a bevy of nuns and priests, Sister Carlotta and Sister Emmanuel leave the Dominican Republic on a tourist boat bound for Newark, New Jersey.

They begin life again at St. Peter's Hospital in New Brunswick.

Sister Emmanuel is a lover of bargains. She finds the newly repaired Welcome Chair outside a Salvation Army store. The chair makes nice squeaks.

She buys it for one dollar and brings it home. She scratches the word "*Bienvenido*" in Spanish into the wood with a pen knife. The chair is the perfect birthday gift for Sister Carlotta.

In the evenings Sister Carlotta gets off her aching feet, and rocks in the
Welcome Chair.

She sips lemon tea and gives butter cookies to young patients who sit in her lap.

Into the night she and Sister Emmanuel laugh and gossip about the doctors.

In the year 2010, Sister Carlotta and Sister Emmanuel leave this earth two
months apart. The Welcome Chair is placed in a rummage sale.

Pearl Basquet's mother grabs it.
She lemon oils its arms, seat, and back until it gleams.

Pearl claims it as her homework chair. She rocks and reads her books, away from her big brother, Cyrus, who makes too much noise.

One morning Pearl's father opens his newspaper.

A terrible earthquake has crippled the country of Haiti.

"I am a doctor," he says. "I must go down and help."

"Can I come?" asks Pearl.

Pearl cannot come. But her father sends back pictures of his emergency clinic set up in a tent by the Red Cross.

When her father comes home he is carrying a small, moving bundle.

In it is a baby boy. His name is Jean-Marie.

Pearl's father tells her, "I took care of Jean-Marie at the clinic. His mama and papa were lost in the earthquake. We are a family now."

Pearl makes her new brother giggle.

"You know what we have to do?" asks Pearl.

"What?" ask Pearl's father and mother.

"Our Welcome Chair needs a new word," says Pearl.

Cyrus chisels "*Byenvini*" below the Spanish "*Bienvenido*."

One Sunday in 2016, in the Basquets' church, Father Fiori announces that a new family has moved to town from a distant land destroyed by war. The family escaped, trudging a hundred miles carrying a baby and an old grandmother. They jammed onto a boat with too many people. They have a ten-year-old girl, says Father Fiori, but her baby sister fell out of the crowded boat and into the ocean and drowned.

"This family needs help," says Father Fiori. "They have nothing."

Pearl and her best friend, Amanda, look at each other.

"I'll give my American Girl doll, Samantha," says Amanda.

Pearl knows what she wants to give. First she has to ask Jean-Marie, since his family's "welcome" was on the chair.

Jean-Marie is now a six-year-old first baseman. He says, "Sure, you bet!"

Pearl and Amanda go to the town library. They find the word they want.

Amanda's father helps whittle in the loopy letters.

Her name is Amira. She sits on a bed in a house trailer that Father Fiori's church rents for them.

She has never seen a rocking chair or an American Girl doll.

Pearl shows her how to rock. Amanda puts Samantha in Amira's arms.

For the first time in many months, Amira smiles.
Those three girls form a perfect shape, like a heart.

AUTHOR'S NOTE

When I was just about ten, my grandmother showed me her drawer of treasures. In it was a diary, written in spidery old German *alte schrift* handwriting by my great-great-grandmother Ruth Seigbert.

To me the faded writing looked like the scratching of chicken feet.

My grandmother translated the words and read them aloud.

The first half of this book is a family memoir based on that diary and my recollection of it—long sleeping in my memory, difficult to confirm or research. The story was left dangling, but now has come to life many years later in a very different America.

What I can confirm is that my great-great-grandfather Sam Seigbert came to America to escape religious conformity. Ruth immigrated because of physical disability and old wives' tales. They changed their first names from the unpronounceable German to "Sam" and "Ruth" to become "more American." My family were shopkeepers in the Midwest. They are buried there. Almost everyone who came to America escaped something—dictators, natural disasters, wars, famine, religious discrimination. On Ellis Island in New York Harbor, Miss Liberty opened her arms to them.

In our current time, there are leaders who would close our doors to the tired and poor who were once welcomed here. Because I disagree with them from the bottom of my heart, I wanted to write about the chair that welcomed members of my family for so long. The trouble was, my grandmother's account ended in 1918. No one knew what happened to the Welcome Chair after that. As a writer I had to find the rest of the story myself. I found that if I looked and listened, I could find twenty real stories.

At a gathering at my daughter's school, the Convent of the Sacred Heart in Connecticut, I met two elderly nuns who had escaped the dictator Trujillo in Santo Domingo in the 1950s. They came to New Jersey as nurses. In 2016, my daughter's best friend helped a local doctor's rescue efforts after the earthquake in Haiti. Another friend sponsored a Syrian family here in my hometown, Stamford. And so, listening and taking notes as writers do, I had a complete book. Providence smiled, and Jerry Pinkney has made it all come alive.

—*Rosemary Wells*

SAMUEL SEIGBERT, ABOUT 1870

ILLUSTRATOR'S NOTE

For more than sixty years of my art-making practices with works heavily based on research, I have amassed an extensive reference library: volumes on nature, American history, as well as on the arts. There are hundreds of books overflowing my studio bookshelves. *The Welcome Chair*, with its warm prose, has emotional depth. It is well written and articulate, which served as a springboard for me to speak to my passion for American history. The text was also a road map to how I would interpret Rosemary Wells's ancestry and the American immigrant story. The handcrafted rocking chair was the connecting line to families and to those that make up this American experience.

The research for this book was daunting, covering a period of time more than two centuries and six settings and locations. Each place required a new set of specific treatment—the time period, its subjects, and their costumes.

The visual challenge was how to maintain a cohesive and consistent look and feel to my art. I decided that executing the illustrations with contour drawing and watercolor washes was the solution. I then created pictures using burnt okra Prismacolor pencils and pastels, similar to the red chalk figurative images of the nineteenth century—drawing being the thread holding together the patchwork quilt of story squared from the 1800s until the present day.

Rosemary and I have our own backstory. We have known each other for more than fifty years. Our friendship, along with my respect and admiration for a fellow bookmaker—and her narrative woven into the national fabric—helped to find my artistic energy.

PRELIMINARY THUMBNAIL SKETCH,
MICRON MARKER ON PAPER

—*Jerry Pinkney*

For Jerry Pinkney, artist extraordinaire
—R. W.

To Rosemary Wells and the American story
—J. P.

———————————————————

The author wishes to thank the Reverend Sam Owen
and the New York Haiti Project for their help with this book.

———————————————————

SIMON & SCHUSTER BOOKS FOR YOUNG READERS
An imprint of Simon & Schuster Children's Publishing Division
1230 Avenue of the Americas, New York, New York 10020
Text © 2021 by Rosemary Wells
Illustrations © 2021 by Jerry Pinkney
Book design by Laurent Linn © 2021 by Simon & Schuster, Inc.
All rights reserved, including the right of reproduction in whole or in part in any form.
SIMON & SCHUSTER BOOKS FOR YOUNG READERS and related marks are trademarks of Simon & Schuster, Inc.
For information about special discounts for bulk purchases, please contact Simon & Schuster Special Sales
at 1-866-506-1949 or business@simonandschuster.com.
The Simon & Schuster Speakers Bureau can bring authors to your live event. For more information or to book an event,
contact the Simon & Schuster Speakers Bureau at 1-866-248-3049 or visit our website at www.simonspeakers.com.
The text for this book was set in Chaparral Pro.
The illustrations for this book were rendered in watercolor, Prismacolor pencil, and pastel.
Manufactured in China
0621 SCP
First Edition
2 4 6 8 10 9 7 5 3 1
Library of Congress Cataloging-in-Publication Data
Names: Wells, Rosemary, author. | Pinkney, Jerry, illustrator.
Title: The Welcome Chair / Rosemary Wells ; illustrated by Jerry Pinkney.
Description: New York : Simon & Schuster Books for Young Readers, 2021. | "A Paula Wiseman Book." | Audience: Ages 4–8. | Audience: Grades 2–3. |
Summary: In this story based on true events, a treasured wooden chair is passed down from family to family,
with each new owner carving the word "welcome" in a new language.
Identifiers: LCCN 2021000043 (print) | LCCN 2021000044 (ebook) | ISBN 9781534429772 (hardcover) | ISBN 9781534429789 (ebook)
Subjects: CYAC: Chairs—Fiction. | Immigrants—Fiction.
Classification: LCC PZ7.W46843 We 2021 (print) | LCC PZ7.W46843 (ebook) | DDC [E]—dc23
LC record available at https://lccn.loc.gov/2021000043
LC ebook record available at https://lccn.loc.gov/2021000044

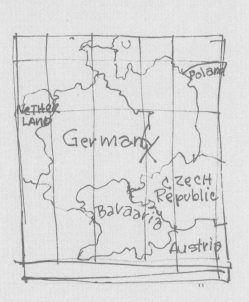

Germany

NeTHER LAND

Poland

Czech Republic

Bavaria

Austria